Just a Postcard Away
ISBN 978-1-7324067-4-2

Ballard Publishing Group, LLC.

This book is dedicated to my niece, Taylor M.,
and all the little boys and girls who dare to
dream big and reach for their goals!

Taylor's Aunt Fran was just about the best aunt a kid could ever have! She gave the best hugs, told the funniest stories and made the best pancakes! One morning, her Aunt Fran came over for a visit. After a nice pancake breakfast, she sat Taylor down and told her that soon she would be going on a long trip.

"Where are you going Aunt Fran?"

"'I've decided to go on an adventure around the world, but first I'm going to a place called Abu Dhabi. It is in the desert, far across the ocean in the United Arab Emirates."

"The desert? Aunt Fran, you can't go! How are you going to get water, and who is going to make me yummy pancakes?"

"Don't worry there is plenty of water in Abu Dhabi, and I'm sure we can find you a substitute pancake maker," Aunt Fran said with a smile. "I'm going to be teaching English to the children who live in Abu Dhabi."

"Why do you need to teach them English, are they babies?"

"No, they are not babies," her aunt laughed. "They just speak a different language. It's called Arabic."

Taylor thought for a minute.

"That's awfully nice of you Aunt Fran, but this sounds like a big job. You are going to need some help. Just wait here one minute, I'll be right back!"

Taylor jumped up and dashed up the stairs. A few minutes later she returned.

"What's all this?" asked Aunt Fran.

"I speak very good English Aunt Fran, so I'm coming to help you. I'm all packed, so when do we leave?"

"Oh Taylor," her aunt cooed, "I can't take you with me. You have to stay here and go to school. You'll be headed to first grade soon and if you leave, your mommy and daddy will surely miss you."

Taylor's eyes began to well with tears. She had to find a way to make her aunt stay. She thought and thought until finally she had a plan.

The next day when her aunt came over for tea, Taylor lumbered into the living room. She was moaning and groaning as if she were in the worst pain of her life. Her body was covered in purples spots from head to toe.

"I think I have the turkey pox!" she whined.

"Oh my!" said Aunt Fran with a slight grin. "You look terrible, but don't you mean the chicken pox."

"No, I mean the turkey pox! I looked it up on the internet. It says they are worse than the chicken pox! I may even have to be quarter-teened. Oh the pain! Please Aunt Fran you have to stay, I don't think I'm going to make it!" said Taylor as she collapsed dramatically into her aunt's arms.

"I see," said Aunt Fran, trying to look concerned as she felt Taylor's forehead. "We can not let you get *quarantined*, maybe we should give you a warm bath to help you feel better."

"Look!" her aunt said, "Your spots are disappearing, I think you are going to be ok!"

Taylor sighed, as she sat in the now purple sea of bubbly bath water.

After lots of thinking and talking it over with her stuffed animal, Trunks, Taylor had a new idea. She decided to write her aunt a note.

Der Ant Fran
Plz do not go to the dsrt. It is
hot and you wil mlt. I wil mis
you vree muj if you mlt.
    If you sta I wil mak YOU
pancaks evree day. Plz sta!

Luv,
Taylor

The next day as they headed to the airport, Taylor handed her aunt the note. Aunt Fran quietly read the note and smiled. She leaned over and hugged Taylor.

"Don't be sad. I am going to miss you too. I promise I will write, I'll send you postcards along the way. It will be as if we are traveling together, I'll always be just a postcard away!"

"Okay," Taylor said softly.

When they arrived at the airport, Taylor hugged her aunt as tears rolled down her cheeks. She stood there watching until her aunt Fran disappeared into the dense crowd of travelers.

A month later, a postcard arrived in the mail. On the cover was a picture of a camel in the desert. Taylor could hardly contain her excitement as she handed her mother the postcard to read. As her mother read, Taylor listened intently to every word.

Marhaba (Mar-ha-ba) Taylor,

That means hello or welcome in Arabic. Trunk
and I have made it to the desert! It is very ho
here, but you will be happy to know that I hav
not melted. I am enjoying teaching Englis
here, and my students are very excited to lear
When I'm not teaching, I enjoy visiting some of th
local sites. Today was a special day, I visited wit
one of my students at her home. She and he
family have a farm. They were so welcomin
We shared a traditional Arabic meal tha
included tabbouleh, fish, dates and hummus. I eve
got to ride a camel. I miss you already, and I can
wait to share more of my travels with you!

Love,

Aunt Fran

Taylor smiled to herself as she imagined what it would be like to ride a camel in the desert. She would be sure to carry lots of water!

Taylor's mom placed the card on a display board in Taylor's room. She was so excited about her postcard that she asked her mother to read it to her almost every day. Soon, she had it memorized.

A few months later, to Taylors delight, another postcard arrived. It had a large tower on the front. Taylor and her mother sat down to read the card together.

Bonjour (Bon-zhur) Taylor,

That means hello in French!

I'm in France, in the city of Paris! I just saw the Eiffel Tower, and I couldn't believe my eyes! It was just exquisite! The Eiffel tower is actually the tallest structure in Paris. It was built in 1889 with the help of a French-man named Gustave Eiffel. Inside you can climb 300 steps to look out over the city! Do you think you could climb that many steps? I can't wait to see you again!

Love,

Aunt Fran

Taylor didn't think, she *knew* she could climb that many steps. She giggled at the thought of running up the steps of the Eiffel Tower and waving to the people below. She couldn't wait to visit Paris for herself one day and give it a try!

Throughout the years many postcards arrived. By the time Taylor was in second grade, she could read all the postcards on her own. One day she received a card with a long wall on the front. She turned it over to read.

Ni Hao (nee-how) Taylor,

That means hello in Mandarin. Today I'm visitir
Beijing China! The front of this postcard shows Th
Great Wall of China, it was built to prever
invasions. Thousands of years ago soldiers eve
marched along this wall. The Great Wall of Chin
is the longest man-made structure in the world!
stretches over 13,000 miles. It's truly an amazir
wonder. I'm thinking of you always!

Love,

Aunt Fran

"I would have made a great soldier," thought Taylor. She smiled as she envisioned herself marching along the wall, leading the other soldiers as they watched for invaders.

Each new post card made Taylor feel closer and closer to her aunt. She couldn't believe that she had tried to stop her aunt from leaving all those years ago. She was having so much fun learning about the world, as her aunt Fran shared her adventures through beautiful picture postcards. Taylor couldn't wait for the day when she could travel the world, and she knew exactly where she wanted to go first.

She reached up and gently removed the postcard that her aunt had sent from Kenya.

Jambo (Jom-bo) Taylor,

I went on safari today in Africa! I'm in a place called the Masai Mara. It lies within the luscious greens and rolling hills of Kenya. I drove through the huge open grasslands where I saw giraffes running free, lions hunting to feed their cubs, and a troop of elephants foraging through the bushes. While out at the street market, I found this post card and it made me think of you. The little girl in the picture is adorned in hand painted Kazuri beads. She looks so full of hopes and dreams. I know you have big dreams too! Always remember you can do and be anything! There is a whole world out here just waiting for you!

Love,

Aunt Fran

She imagined the Masai Mara in all of its beauty. Yes, this postcard was her absolute favorite!

Taylor's imagination ran wild as she thought about the beautiful country of Kenya and all of her wonderful postcards. Soon she heard a knock on her bedroom door.

"Come in, Mommy." she said
When the door opened, Taylor's eyes grew wide and a smile as big as the ocean spread across her face.

A woman who was covered from head to toe in purple spots and carrying a stuffed elephant walked into her room.

As she hugged Taylor, she whispered softly, "I think I have the turkey pox now too," and they both giggled.

Taylor knew right then and there that even though she may not ever get another postcard, her adventures had only just begun.

Made in the USA
Monee, IL
05 September 2019